Questions and Answers: Countries

Lebanon

A Question and Answer Book

by Mary Englar

Consultant:
Christopher Rose
Outreach and Study Abroad Coordinator
Center for Middle Eastern Studies
The University of Texas at Austin

Capstone
press

Mankato, Minnesota

Fact Finders is published by Capstone Press
151 Good Counsel Drive, P.O. Box 669, Mankato, Minnesota 56002.
www.capstonepress.com

Library of Congress Cataloging-in-Publication Data
Englar, Mary.
    Lebanon : a question and answer book / by Mary Englar.
    p. cm.—(Fact Finders. Questions and answers : Countries)
    Includes bibliographical references and index.
    ISBN–13: 978–0–7368–6771–9 (hardcover)
    ISBN–10: 0–7368–6771–6 (hardcover)
    1. Lebanon—Juvenile literature. I. Title.
DS80.E53 2007
956.92—dc22   2006028238

Summary: Describes the geography, history, economy, and culture of Lebanon in a
    question-and-answer format.

Editorial Credits
Silver Editions, editorial, design, photo research and production; Kia Adams, set designer;
    Maps.com, cartographer

Photo Credits
Alamy/Bill Lyons, 13; Char Abumansoor, 7; Helene Rogers, 27; IML Image Group Ltd, 9;
    Janine Wiedel Photolibrary, 17; Paul Doyle, cover (foreground)
AP/Wide World Photos/Adnan Hajj Ali, 19; Dalia Khamissy, 15, 23
Capstone Press Archives, 29 (money)
Corbis/Michael Nicholson, cover (background); Sygma/Attar Mahar, 20
Getty Images Inc./AFP/Karim Jaafar, 18; AFP/Ramzi Haidar, 21
One Mile Up, Inc., 29 (flag)
Peter Arnold/Stewart Innes, 4
Shutterstock/Elke Dennis, 25
SuperStock, 11; age fotostock, 1

1 2 3 4 5 6 12 11 10 09 08 07

Table of Contents

Features

Where is Lebanon?

Lebanon is in the Middle East area of southwestern Asia. It's a tiny country, smaller than the U.S. state of Connecticut.

Lebanon's coastline runs for 140 miles (225 kilometers) along the Mediterranean Sea. The narrow coastal plain has hot, humid summers.

Much of the country is mountainous. Snow caps the high peaks in winter.

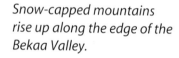

Snow-capped mountains rise up along the edge of the Bekaa Valley.

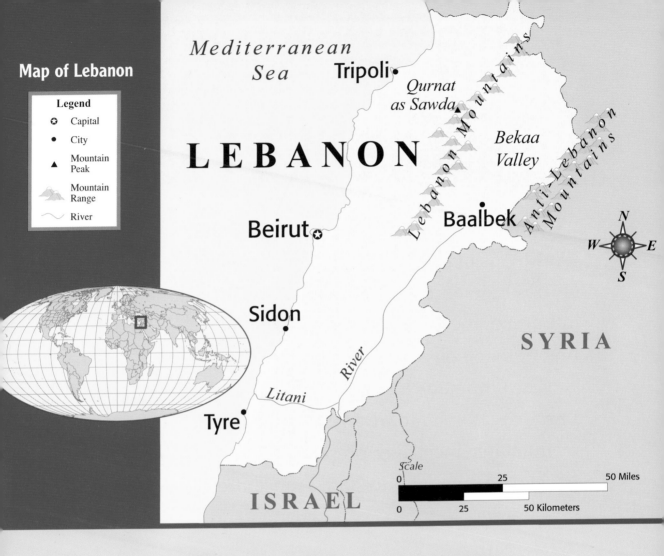

Map of Lebanon

Legend
- ✪ Capital
- • City
- ▲ Mountain Peak
- Mountain Range
- ～ River

Mediterranean Sea

Tripoli•

Qurnat as Sawda▲

LEBANON

Lebanon Mountains

Bekaa Valley

Anti-Lebanon Mountains

Beirut✪

Baalbek•

Sidon•

Litani
River

SYRIA

Tyre•

N
W ✦ E
S

Scale
0 — 25 — 50 Miles
0 — 25 — 50 Kilometers

ISRAEL

The Bekaa Valley lies between the Lebanon and the Anti-Lebanon Mountains. The Litani River runs for 90 miles (145 kilometers) through the valley. Farmers use the Litani River to **irrigate** their vegetable and grain crops.

When did Lebanon become a country?

Lebanon became a country in 1943. Before World War I (1914–1918), Lebanon was part of the Ottoman **Empire**. When the war began in Europe, the Ottomans and Germany fought together.

The Ottomans lost the war. The Ottoman Empire was split apart. In 1920, France took over an area including present-day Syria, Israel, Lebanon, and Jordan. France drew new borders to try to keep Lebanon and Syria apart.

Fact!

Lebanese Christians and Muslims fought a civil war from 1975 to 1990. Religious and political differences continue to cause problems in and around Lebanon today.

The Lebanese people have been fighting for their freedom for many years.

Many Lebanese were unhappy with the French **occupation**. Lebanese **Muslims** wanted to join with Syria. Christians wanted Lebanon to be its own country. Both wanted independence from France. In 1943, the Lebanese government declared independence.

What type of government does Lebanon have?

Lebanon is a **republic**. Lebanon's first leaders agreed to divide government positions between Lebanon's religious groups. Every four years, the people vote for the 128 **representatives** in the National Assembly. Half of the representatives are Christians and half are Muslims.

Every six years, the National Assembly chooses a Christian president. The president then chooses a Muslim **prime minister**. The government tries to represent everyone, but problems often arise.

Fact!

All Lebanese men may vote at age 21. Lebanese women can vote, but only if they have completed elementary school.

The Grand Serail building contains Lebanon's government offices in the capital, Beirut.

Syria has played an important role in Lebanon's government since the Lebanese Civil War. Many Lebanese people have protested against the influence of Syria and other nations. The Lebanese want to be more independent of other nations.

What kind of housing does Lebanon have?

Most Lebanese live in modern apartments in coastal cities. New concrete apartment buildings are built next to old houses. These houses have arched windows and balconies.

In the mountains, people live in villages near their farms. Rural houses often have tile roofs and stone walls.

Where do people live in Lebanon?

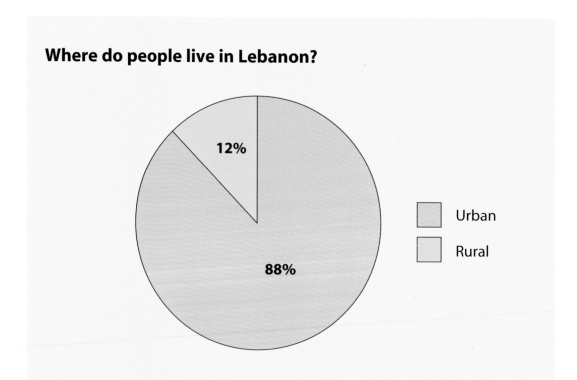

12%

88%

Urban

Rural

Beirut shows scars from past fighting as well as hope for the future as people construct new buildings.

The civil war destroyed much of Lebanon's housing. Many farmers moved from small mountain villages to the city to escape the fighting. The government has built many new apartment buildings, but some people still do not have homes.

What are Lebanon's forms of transportation?

Lebanon's cities have many forms of transportation. Cars, taxis, and buses clog Beirut's streets. Beirut has so many vehicles that traffic jams happen every day. Air pollution is a growing problem in the city.

Paved roads connect most towns in Lebanon. Many people take buses and taxis to nearby towns and vacation spots. Lebanon is so small that no town is more than a few hours away.

Fact!

Taxis are expensive in Lebanon's cities. Because of this, some people share rides in taxis called servees. These old cars can carry four or five passengers.

Beirut is a busy port for many countries in the Middle East. Many ships loaded with goods dock here each day.

Lebanon's ports have served countries in the Middle East for thousands of years. The cities of Beirut, Tripoli, and Sidon are the largest ports. Ships bring trade goods bound for Syria, Jordan, and Iraq.

What are Lebanon's major industries?

Most Lebanese people work in the service industry. They work in hotels, shops, and restaurants. Some work at ski resorts in the mountains.

Construction and factory work employ some Lebanese. Construction workers repair damage from wars and fighting. Factories produce cement, food, and clothing.

What does Lebanon import and export?	
Imports	**Exports**
oil	jewelry
cars	chemicals
medicine	fruit
clothing	construction materials
meat	electric machinery
live animals	textiles
fabrics	paper

A ski lift takes tourists to the peak at the Faraya-Mzaar resort. Most Lebanese people work in tourist or service industries.

Only 10 percent of Lebanon's people are farmers. Bananas, citrus fruits, olives, and wheat grow well in different parts of the country. In the mountains, some farmers grow grapes to make wine.

What is school like in Lebanon?

Public schools are free for all children from grade school through high school. About half of Lebanon's schools are public. The rest are private schools.

Lebanese parents send their children to private schools if possible. Classes are smaller at private schools. Some public school classes have as many as 40 students.

Fact!

All Lebanese children study Arabic in school. Formal Arabic is different from the language they speak at home. Most students also study French and English.

Most primary schools in Lebanon require students to wear uniforms.

Lebanese children begin school when they are six. Grade school lasts five years. Students have different teachers for each subject. They study math, history, geography, and science.

Most students continue on to intermediate school. After four years, they take an exam for high school. High school lasts three years.

What are Lebanon's favorite sports and games?

Soccer is the most popular sport in Lebanon. People of all ages enjoy watching and playing the game. Teams from different clubs and cities compete for the country's top honor each spring.

Lebanon's beaches and mountains offer many other sports activities. Visitors can swim, sail, or windsurf in the Mediterranean Sea. Six mountain resorts are only an hour away from the coast. People can ski and snowboard there in the winter.

Fact!

Fadi el-Khatib has earned his place as the best forward for the Lebanese National Basketball team.

Lebanese soccer player Hayssam Atwi (in white) slides in to block a player during the 2004 Olympics.

Basketball is also popular in Lebanon. The national team plays against other teams from Asia in the International Basketball Association. In 2005, the team won a silver medal in the championship games.

What are the traditional art forms in Lebanon?

The Lebanese love music and dancing. Traditional musicians play a drum, a flute, and an *oud*, a type of stringed instrument, at weddings and parties. Musicians and singers perform at music festivals every year.

Marcel Khalife is an expert *oud* player from Lebanon. Khalife **composes** music based on Arabic poetry. He gives concerts all over the world.

Fact!

Fairuz is the most famous Lebanese singer. She sings folk songs, religious songs, and pop songs. Fairuz has been giving concerts all over the world for more than 50 years.

Many people perform the dabke *at traditional weddings and other joyful occasions. Dabke is an Arabic word that means "feet stomping."*

People in most every city and village dance the *dabke*, a Lebanese folk dance, as part of celebrations. One dancer will lead a line of dancers in a series of steps and jumps. Often, everyone joins in the dance and follows the leader.

What holidays do people in Lebanon celebrate?

Most of Lebanon's holidays are religious. Muslims **fast** for a month during Ramadan. At the end of Ramadan, they celebrate Eid al-Fitr. Families visit relatives and enjoy sweet pastries.

Christians celebrate Easter dinner with their families. Many travel back to their home villages. They might eat cakes called *maamoul* that have walnuts or dates.

What other holidays do people in Lebanon celebrate?

New Year's Day
Labor Day
Martyr's Day
Christmas
Eid al-Adha
Prophet Muhammad's Birthday

Military parades, speeches, and fireworks are all ways that Lebanon celebrates its freedom on Independence Day.

The Lebanese celebrate their Independence Day on November 22. Lebanon won its freedom from France on that day in 1943. Like the Fourth of July in the United States, most people have the day off.

What are the traditional foods of Lebanon?

Before meals, Lebanese cooks serve **meze**. Meze includes spicy vegetable dips, olives, salads, and pickled vegetables. Families gather around a large table and dip bread into each dish.

Fresh bread is served at every meal. The Lebanese use soft, flat bread instead of silverware. They tear off a piece of bread and use it to scoop up the food.

Fact!

Shawarma is chicken or lamb grilled on a turning spit. Street cafes in Lebanon often sell shawarma sandwiches. Strips of meat are wrapped in flat bread. Cucumbers, onions, tomatoes, and garlic sauce top the warm meat.

Tabbouleh is a traditional salad from Lebanon. It has cracked wheat, tomatoes, parsley, mint, and other ingredients.

Main meals are usually grilled chicken or lamb. Meatballs called *kibbeh* are a favorite. They are made from lamb and crushed wheat. Families enjoy grapes, oranges, or melon for dessert.

What is family life like in Lebanon?

Most Lebanese families live in large cities. Families are small, but relatives often live nearby. Young adults live with their parents until they get married.

Rural families are often larger and work together. Grandparents, cousins, and other relatives often live in the same house or village.

What are the ethnic backgrounds of people in Lebanon?

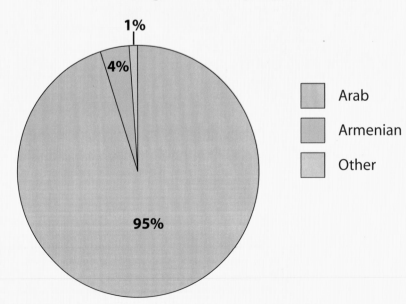

1%
4%
95%

Arab
Armenian
Other

Though they may live far apart, many Lebanese families come together for celebrations at least once a year.

Many Lebanese people **emigrated**, or left the country, during the civil war. They miss their families and try to return to Lebanon every year for a visit. Relatives welcome them back with food and celebrations.

Lebanon Fast Facts

Official name:

Lebanese Republic

Population:

3,874,050 people

Land area:

*3,950 square miles
(10,230 square kilometers)*

Capital city:

Beirut

**Average annual
precipitation:**

33 inches (84 centimeters)

Languages:

*Arabic (official), French,
English, Armenian*

**Average January
temperature (Beirut):**

*56 degrees Fahrenheit
(13 degrees Celsius)*

Natural resources:

limestone, iron ore, salt, water

**Average July
temperature (Beirut):**

*81 degrees Fahrenheit
(27 degrees Celsius)*

Religions:

Muslim	*60%*
Christian	*39%*
Other	*1%*

Money and Flag

Money:

The main unit of Lebanese money is the pound. One pound equals 100 piastres. In 2006, one U.S. dollar equaled 1,520 pounds. One Canadian dollar equaled 1,327 pounds.

Flag:

The Lebanese flag has red and white stripes. In the center of the white stripe is a green cedar tree. The cedar tree represents the ancient Cedars of Lebanon. It also stands for strength.

Learn to Speak Arabic

Arabic is the official language of Lebanon. Learn to speak some Arabic words and phrases below.

English	Arabic	Pronunciation
hello	marhaba	mahr-HAH-bah
good-bye	ma'a salaama	MAH suh-LAH-mah
please	min fadlak	min FAHD-lahk
thank you	shukran	SHUH-krahn
What is your name?	Shu ismak?	Shoo is-MAHK?
My name is _____	Ismi_____	IS-mi _____
yes	na'am	NAHM
no	la	LAH

Glossary

compose (kuhm-POHZ)—to write music

emigrate (EM-uh-grayt)—to leave one's own country to live in another one

empire (EM-pire)—a group of countries that have the same ruler

fast (FAST)—to give up eating for a period of time for religious reasons; Lebanese Muslims fast during Ramadan.

irrigate (IHR-uh-gayt)—to supply water for crops using ditches or pipes

meze (ME-zay)—appetizers served before dinner

Muslim (MUHZ-luhm)—a follower of the religion of Islam; Muslims believe in one god, Allah, and that Muhammad is his prophet.

occupation (awk-yuh-PAY-shuhn)—taking over and controlling another country with an army

prime minister (PRIME MIN-uh-ster)—a person in charge of the government in some countries

representative (rep-ruh-ZEN-tuh-tiv)—someone who is elected to speak for others in government

republic (ri-PUHB-lik)—government with officials elected by the people

Internet Sites

FactHound offers a safe, fun way to find Internet sites related to this book. All of the sites on FactHound have been researched by our staff.

Here's how:
1. Visit *www.facthound.com*
2. Choose your grade level.
3. Type in this book ID **0736867716** for age-appropriate sites. You may also browse subjects by clicking on letters, or by clicking on pictures and words.
4. Click on the **Fetch It** button.

FactHound will fetch the best sites for you!

Read More

Conley, Kate A. *Lebanon*. The Countries. Edina, Minn.: Abdo, 2004.

Goldstein, Margaret J. *Lebanon in Pictures.* Visual Geography Series. Minneapolis: Lerner, 2005.

Skahill, Carolyn M. *A Historical Atlas of Lebanon*. New York: Rosen, 2004.

Willis, Terri. *Lebanon*. Enchantment of the World. Second Series. New York: Children's Press, 2005.

Index